Second Chance

by

Alison Prince

Illustrated by Alison Prince

First published in 2000 in Great Britain by
Barrington Stoke Ltd
www.barringtonstoke.co.uk

Reprinted 2002, 2004, 2005

ISBN 1-842991-94-9

Printed in Great Britain by Bell & Bain Ltd

A Note from the Author – Alison Prince

One of my first ever stories was about a ghost that went round popping balloons. I wrote it in a very boring office where I was supposed to be a trainee telegraphist (a sort of early computer operator). I hadn't clocked that the machine I was working on could send what I wrote to other people's machines. Unknown to me, my story was coming out in the boss's office. He came bursting in with a face like thunder. "You're not here to write *stories*," he screamed, "you're here to copy what you're given." I got the sack, of course.

I didn't care. I'd learned to type by that time, which was dead useful. I got sacked from a lot more jobs, and after a bit, I gave up trying to do anything except write stories. They're hard work, but at least I'm never bored.

Contents

Chapter 1
Thrown Out

The Council said we'd have to leave the house. People had been complaining about the noise and the buggies in the garden and Steve's van and the greyhounds. Steve says he'll win a fortune one of these days betting on the dogs, but it hasn't happened yet.

The men who own the greyhounds only want the ones that win the races. The rest

get put down or given away. Steve can never say no to a nice dog – that's why we've ended up with seven.

Steve isn't my Dad. He moved in after my Dad moved out ten years ago, but he and Mum get on fine. She doesn't mind the dogs. When you've got eight kids, I suppose you don't notice a few greyhounds.

I'm Ross, I'm the eldest. Then there's Kate, who's 13. After that, there's Tim and the twins, Jinty and Callum, and the little ones, Patsy, Paul and wee Eric. And at the time when the Council threw us out, Mum was going to have another one.

They offered us this flat in a tower block. We left the dogs at home and went to look at it, but we all hated it. Steve said his van would get nicked down there where he couldn't watch it, but that was just an excuse. You'd have to be mad to nick Steve's van.

Kate said, "You can't go in and out, can you?"

She was right – there was nothing outside except sky and a very long drop. And we liked having the doors open so dogs and children could be in and out all the time.

The woman from the Council said we couldn't pick and choose, but Mum said, "When you can't choose you might as well be dead. And this isn't the place for us."

So the Council woman put the top back on her pen and closed her notebook. And that was it. We were to leave by the end of the week.

We were a bit quiet going home.

Tim said, "Well, where are we going to
live?"

Nobody answered. Paul was bawling
because he wanted to ride in the lift. We
told him it was broken which was true – but
he didn't care. Mum was walking ahead,

5

carrying Eric. She never used the buggies people gave us.

Our house was on the edge of the council estate, quite near the sea. If you went through the gap in the fence you were out on the dunes, all sand and rough grass. You couldn't push a buggy through it. That's why the buggies rotted away in the garden.

"Where are we going to *live?*" Tim asked again.

He's the worrying kind, like my Dad was.

Mum said, "In the old café."

We all ran to catch up with her.

Steve said, "You mean the place down by the sewage works?"

"That's right," said Mum. "I've been thinking about it. We can pay a bit of rent

if anyone asks. It's a crime to have a big place like that standing empty."

"But it's falling to bits," Tim said. "All the windows have got boards nailed over them."

Steve grinned. He's got a missing front tooth, which makes him look a real tough. I think he likes it that way. "We can soon shift a few boards," he said. "Can't we, Ross?"

"Sure," I said. "After work tomorrow, OK?"

I'm fifteen and still at school, sort of, only I've got this job at the Tyre and Battery place.

The dogs came leaping out when we opened the door. My favourite is Hokum. He's black with white toes and he sleeps on my bed.

"We're going to have a new home," Kate told them. "You'll love it."

Jinty said, "We'll love it, too."

Somehow we all got excited then. It was a year or two since our last move and we'd been getting a bit bored. Mum cooked up a pile of sausages and mash and a big pot of beans. Then her brothers, Spike and Danny, turned up. They'd found a new door for Steve's van because the other one got bashed in.

When they heard about the café they went out for some beer and coke, and crisps for the kids, and it all turned into a party. We had the CD player on and everyone was dancing. The neighbours banged on the wall like they always did.

"Let them bang," said Mum. She was dancing as well even though she was so big with the baby coming. "We'll soon be gone."

Chapter 2
The Café

The next night, Steve parked the van on the weedy tarmac and we got out and looked at the café. The moon was full and we could see the long grass growing over its wooden steps. It was about the size of a village hall, only it was built out over the sea like a pier.

"If there's holes in the floor, we'll fall through and get wet," I said.

Steve was getting tools out of the van.
"Only one way to find out," he said. "Get in
there and look. Take this."

He handed me a hammer and a couple of
tyre levers. Then he reached in for a torch
and a long wrecking bar with a forked end.

Close to, the place looked a real mess.
The paint was peeling off right down to the

wood and the usual seaside rubbish lay about – cans and bits of plastic and broken glass. There was a torn poster on the wall.

"Was this a dance hall, then?" I asked. I was ramming a tyre lever under a plank.

"*Café Dansant*, they called it," said Steve. "Dance floor in the middle, tables and chairs round the edge. My Gran used to come here. She thought it was great." He prised a board off with the wrecking bar.

When we'd got the door clear, Steve put his shoulder to it and shoved. It didn't move.

"Bolted from inside," he said. He knocked the rest of the broken glass out of the window next to it and climbed in.

I handed him the hammer and heard him bashing at the bolts. Then he pulled the door open and stood there with his gap-toothed grin.

"Come in," he said. "Welcome to our new home."

Inside, it was pitch dark. It smelt weird. Damp and rotten, with a musty reek of seagull muck, but sort of perfumed as well. Like one of those big shops where they sell lipstick and stuff, only very faint and stale.

Steve shone the torch round. The place looked like the entrance to a cinema, with toilets on either side and a box office. In front of us there was a row of glass doors.

We pushed through and found ourselves in what looked like a ballroom. The torch lit up the edge of a gallery that went round three sides. Then Steve swept the beam across the stage. The back wall had a zigzag sunburst design on it, pink and black and gold.

"Wait till Jinty sees that," I said. Jinty was sure she was going to be a pop star, so she was desperate to get on any stage.

Steve was walking over to a door in the corner. I started to follow him, then noticed the floor was damp and gritty under my feet. I looked up to see where the wet had come from and saw this massive great hole in the roof. The girders were still there.

Where they crossed in the middle, a mirror-ball was hanging – one of those things that throw sparkles of light round the walls and the ceiling. It looked really strange, as if the café had a moon of its own, as well as the one up there in the sky.

The next moment, I nearly died of fright.

Someone was close behind me. So close, I thought he was going to put his fingers on my neck. I spun round – but there was nobody there. One of the glass doors was closing quietly, all by itself. I went to find Steve, quick.

He was in the kitchen at the back of the building, behind the stage. "Look at this!" he said. "Sinks, draining board, everything. And the taps work."

"Steve," I said. "There's someone here."

"Oh, hell," said Steve. "Where?"

"I think he went through the glass doors. Someone did."

"Better take a look," said Steve.

I followed him back across the empty floor. The glass doors were stiff to push open. Steve shone the torch round, then looked in the toilets labelled LADIES' POWDER ROOM and GENTLEMEN. I couldn't have done it. What if someone was in there, waiting to jump out?

"Not a soul," he said. "You were seeing things."

"I saw the door move," I said. "I know I did." I still had the feeling someone was watching me.

"Come on, Ross," Steve said. "Don't be daft. We've just broken into the place, haven't we? It's been empty for years. There can't be anyone here."

I didn't say any more. But I knew there was.

We went back into the kitchen and Steve hauled the back door open. Outside, there was a narrow balcony like a ship's deck, with a

railing all round it. The moon was making a
bright path across the sea.

"Terrific, isn't it," said Steve. "Good old
Cathy. What a brilliant idea, coming here."

Cathy was my Mum. I found I was thinking about her as Steve went round pushing at the railings, checking they were safe. She was so strong and skinny, apart from the bulge the baby made, and her hair was dark and curly. You'd never think she was forty-two.

We nailed some of the planks back across the door to keep intruders out, then chucked the tools in the van.

"We'll move in tomorrow," Steve said as he started the engine. "Spike and Danny will give us a hand, it won't take long."

I took a last look back. The front of the café was in shadow from the moon above it, but someone was standing there. A boy not much older than me, 16, perhaps, wearing a white T-shirt.

Watching us.

Chapter 3
The Boy

I stayed off work the next day to give a hand with the move. They never minded if I didn't turn up, they just thought I was putting in a day at school.

The café looked worse by daylight. There were patches of black mould on the walls and the floor was littered with chunks of fallen plaster and rotten wood. Sunlight was shining through the hole in the roof

now, but the place was still pretty dark under the galleries. It was pitch black in the toilets and changing rooms where there were no windows. The electricity was off.

The kids didn't mind. They thought it was great. They rushed in and out and up and down the stairs. Tim started collecting bits of wood and plaster from the floor and chucking them in the sea. Mum was sweeping and cleaning. Jinty was on the stage, tap-dancing. At least, that's what she called it.

We'd shut the greyhounds in the old house while we were shifting things, because they'd get in the way. When Danny and Steve came with the last van load of stuff, they said they'd left Kate behind to walk the dogs over. So I said I'd go and meet her.

I started down the wooden steps – and the boy I'd seen last night was there again.

I half saw him from the corner of my eye. White shirt, red hair. Then he was gone. I looked back as I set off across the dunes, but there was no sign of him.

When Kate came towards me with the seven dogs running and jumping all round her, it was weird somehow. I seemed to be a stranger, seeing them for the first time. I wondered if that was how the boy with red hair was seeing us.

He was there again when we got back. I kept getting this glimpse of red hair and a white T-shirt, but if I tried to look at him properly, he'd disappear.

It couldn't have been one of us I was seeing, because there's no red hair in our family. Kate and I are mousy like our dad, and so is Tim, only his is wavy. And the little ones have all got dark, curly hair, same as Mum and Steve.

We had an even better party that night. Mum's sisters came, and her brother Liam, as well as Spike and Danny. They brought their wives and husbands and children and friends. Steve's mates from the dog track turned up too, with several crates of beer.

We couldn't use the CD player because there was no electricity, but that was OK. Steve played his banjo and Spike had brought his accordion and one of the dog men turned out to be great on the fiddle. (The musical sort, I mean.) We had lamps and candles and the gas stove, so it was fine. And nobody banged on the wall.

The little ones fell asleep like puppies on whatever beds and mattresses they chose, but the rest of us kept on partying until daylight started to show through the hole in the roof.

I knew where I wanted to sleep. I'd put a camp bed out on the balcony behind the

kitchen. I was too tired to take my clothes off, so I just lay down with a blanket over me. Hokum came too and curled up beside me. I thought I'd go to sleep at once but I didn't. I lay there looking at the sky getting lighter over the sea and hearing the birds start to sing.

I was getting warm under the blanket. My eyes closed. Then someone said, *"What are you lot doing here?"*

I gasped. I was awake in a flash, sitting up. And there was the boy, leaning on the rail, looking down at the water. The rising sun made his red hair look like a halo of fire.

In that instant, I was terrified he'd fall. I don't know why. I knew the railing was safe and I hadn't been scared when the children had climbed on it, but this was different.

I said aloud, "Be careful."

Hokum glanced up, wondering who I was talking to. I knew he couldn't see the boy, or he'd have barked.

The boy turned his head and looked at me. *"Too late,"* he said.

His voice was in my own mind, like a dream.

I asked, "What do you mean?" and my voice sounded stupidly loud.

He didn't answer. I shut my eyes for a moment against the dazzle of the sun and when I looked again, he wasn't there.

****

When I woke, it was midday. The door to the kitchen was open. Hokum looked out of it and then came to join me, wagging his tail.

I patted him and said, "Been out, have you?"

Kate heard me. She came and leaned against the rail where the boy had been. "It's nice here, isn't it," she said. I was too full of thinking about the boy to answer, so she said again, "Isn't it?" Then she looked at me and asked, "What's the matter?"

"You won't believe this," I said. "It's going to sound mad." And I told her about the boy.

"It must be a ghost," she said.

I frowned. I'd always thought ghosts were grey, wispy things that floated about in castles.

"I'll make some coffee," said Kate.

And left me to think about the red-haired boy.

Chapter 4
Zac

That evening we were all wiped out after two nights of partying and the move, and Mum went off to bed in the upstairs bar quite early. She said if anyone disturbed her, there'd be hell to pay.

Steve had gone to a dog race. We all hoped he was lucky, seeing that we'd run out of everything and needed to hit the supermarket.

Kate and I went round shushing the little ones. Not that they were making much noise, just a bit giggly about having so many sleeping places to choose from.

Kate said, "If your ghost comes, you're to call me. I want to see it."

"He isn't an it," I said, "He's a him. I mean he's sort of real."

"Real but dead," Kate said.

I suppose she was right. I meant to stay awake, but once I was curled up with Hokum, I fell asleep.

"*You're still here, then,*" he said.

I thought I was dreaming. I heard myself say, "Yes, still here."

The boy didn't answer. I opened my eyes and saw him in the moonlight, perched like a

big bird on the railing. Again, I was in a panic
that he'd fall.

He said, *"You don't have to worry. It can't
happen again."*

I thought, what can't? But then I knew.
In a different kind of dream, I saw him
under the water, drifting in the tide. His
eyes were open and his red hair flowed

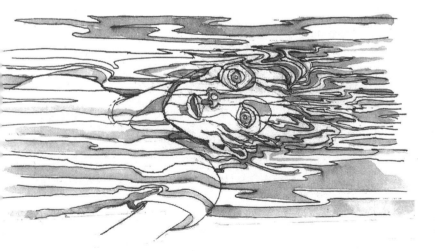

round his head like fine seaweed. Men were coming in a rowing boat, and there was a small crowd of people standing on the beach, some of them weeping.

For a moment, the shock of it left me fighting for breath, as if the sea had poured into my lungs as well as his. The boy was so real. I hated the idea of him being down there in the sea, a drowned thing.

I wanted him to be alive.

He was watching me. His hands were loosely clasped between his knees. His feet, propped against the railing, were in old trainers. *"I'm sorry,"* he said.

"But how did it happen?" I burst out. *"Why did you fall?"* I knew now that I didn't have to speak aloud.

He shrugged one shoulder. Then he said, *"I chose wrong. Stupid."*

I didn't understand. I thought of what Mum had said to the Council woman, 'When you can't choose, you might as well be dead'.

Then it hit me. The boy had chosen to die.

****

Kate got herself and the kids organised for school the next day. She was keen on school, she said she needed to pass her exams.

I went to work – it was pay day. I hadn't earned much because I'd missed two days, but it was better than nothing.

Steve hadn't been lucky, and he'd come home skint. He'd met a man who wanted a chicken shed shifted, so that made him a few quid.

When we got home, Kate and I went shopping for some food. We were hardly out of the café when she said, "I found out who your ghost is."

"Go on?" I tried to sound casual, but I was prickling with interest.

"His name's Zac." Kate was full of excitement. "Zachary Morris. His parents owned the café, years ago. They'd been professional dancers like on telly, they'd won medals and stuff. Ted and Babsy Morris, they were called. The girls at school were talking about it."

"So what happened?" I asked.

"It's a bit sad, really," Kate said. "He was drowned. People say it was suicide. I don't know why – I couldn't ask much. They'd only started on about it because they'd heard about us moving into the café."

I nodded. We got a bad time at school because of the way we lived. The other kids call us gipsies and scroungers. I don't know how Kate puts up with it.

I said, "Did he have brothers and sisters?"

"Don't think so," said Kate, "nobody mentioned any. They said he was a bit weird. On his own a lot."

I wished the boy called Zac was with us so I could ask him, but I had the feeling he couldn't leave the café. It seemed as if he was stuck there, waiting for a second chance that would never come.

Chapter 5
The Baby

When Kate and I got back with the shopping, Steve was playing football with the children on the dunes.

I went to find Mum. She was lying in the big bed in the upstairs bar. Light from the sea outside rippled across the ceiling.

I said, "Are you all right?"

"Dead tired," she said, not moving.

It wasn't like Mum. I wondered if the baby had started coming.

"Shall I go and phone?" I asked. There was a phone box on the main road, about half a mile away.

Mum smiled. "It's all right, love," she said. "The baby's not due for a couple of weeks yet. I just need a rest."

I asked if she'd like a cup of tea and she said she would.

Kate and I cooked spaghetti for everyone, then Steve went out again with his chicken shed money.

"I'm really going to be lucky this time," he said.

We washed up, then Kate sat down with her homework. I went out on the balcony.

The setting sun was down at the sea's edge, glowing red.

"Zac," I said, *"Why did you do it?"*

But he wasn't there. I sat down on my camp bed and leaned my head back on the wall. I shut my eyes and thought about Zac and his parents.

Ted and Babsy Morris. I could see them, practising a dance in the empty café to music from some old plastic record. She would have tight-permed hair, plump arms, little feet in high heels going quick-quick in between his shiny black shoes. And where was Zac?

"My Dad used to burn the rubbish on the beach," Zac said. *"He wouldn't pay the Council to take it away. And they wouldn't do it free because the café was a business, not a private house. All these bits of black stuff*

flew about and the smell made you sick. I'd just left school and he wanted me to run the café. He said I owed him that for bringing me up. He wrote it all down, what I'd cost him, and gave it to me. Like a bill."

I couldn't believe it. I said, *"He must have been off his head."*

"He never wanted children," Zac said. *"He told me. Said he might have been famous."* After a bit, he added, *"Everything hurt. Everything I saw or heard, even my own thoughts. When I woke in the morning, I didn't want to know."*

It was hard to imagine. I mean, I get depressed sometimes, but there's always something you can enjoy or get a laugh out of.

"You lot like each other, don't you?" said Zac. *"I wish I belonged with you."*

"I wish you did, too," I said. *"I wish you were my brother."* And I really meant it.

"The sea was all right," said Zac. *"The sea and the sky. I thought I'd be part of all that. But I'm not."*

I wanted to put my hand on his shoulder or something – but I was never going to be able to touch him. *"It can't go on like this,"* I said. *"Something's got to happen."*

And at that moment, I heard Mum calling from the room above. "Ross," she said, "are you there?"

There was something about her voice that had me on my feet at once.

****

A couple of minutes later, I was biking down to the phone box, with Hokum leaping beside me. I rang the midwife, Mrs Green.

She said she'd be on her way. Mum hated hospitals, she'd never go in them. She always had her babies at home.

When Mrs Green arrived, I took her upstairs.

Mum looked sort of apologetic. "I've never been early with a baby before," she said.

"You've never been forty-two before," said Mrs Green. "But never you mind, my dear, you're going to be fine. Now, let's have a look."

And she sent Kate and me to go and put the kettle on.

We were pretty used to babies being born. There'd be a long wait, then you'd hear that first spluttering cry and know it had arrived. I went out on the balcony to

tell Zac why I'd had to rush off. I hoped he didn't mind.

He wasn't there. His voice didn't sound in my mind and there was nothing to see except the water and the fading light of the sky. Everything seemed very empty.

It was a much longer wait than usual. I could see candlelight flickering through the window of Mum's room upstairs. I lit the gas lamp and carried it up.

Mrs Green was sitting by the bed and her hands were working on something that looked like a lump of dough. She was blowing into it through a rubber tube and I saw with a shock that it was the baby. It was a greyish colour and it lay very still. Mum was staring at it and her eyes looked huge and dark. Her hair was damp, as if she'd been sweating.

Mrs Green looked up at her. "I'm sorry, dear," she said. "I'm afraid this wee boy hasn't made it."

Mum turned her face away and began to cry.

I found that my fists were clenched. *"Please,"* I said silently. *"Oh, please."* I didn't know who I was asking, or what for, but I so much wanted the tiny, blue-grey feet that hung over the midwife's apron to be pink and alive. *"Oh, please."*

Even now, it gives me the shivers to remember this. I saw the baby's chest move. It wasn't much, no more than a kind of quiver, but Mrs Green saw it, too, and said, "Come on, darling. Come on."

In the next minute, he gave a little spluttering cough and began to cry.

Mum gasped through her tears and pushed herself up from the pillows – and Kate came in cheerfully.

"Oh, good," she said. "Is it a boy or a girl?"

"A fine wee boy," said Mrs Green, still busy with the baby. "And I reckon we all need a nice cup of tea."

****

Later, after Kate had gone to bed, I went in to see Mum. The midwife had gone, and Mum was lying with the baby in the crook of her arm. My heart gave a sudden thump. He had red hair. Not much of it, just a fine, silky covering – but bright, coppery red. And a familiar presence was strong in the room.

"Isn't he amazing?" said Mum. "Wherever did this marvellous colour come from? We'll have to think of a really nice name for him."

"But he's Zac," I said, hardly realising I spoke aloud. Zac was real and alive, the same person I knew, but changed, given a new start. A second chance.

"Zac," said Mum. "Zachary. Yes, that's nice."

Steve came running up the stairs. He crouched beside Mum and kissed her. "Are you all right?" he asked. "Kate left a note on the table, said it had been touch and go."

"I'm fine," Mum said. "And just look at your new son, isn't he beautiful!"

Steve stroked the baby's head gently. Then he glanced up at Mum and grinned.

"He brought me luck, anyway," he said. "And how." He hauled a fat roll of notes out of his pocket and tucked it into the baby's shawl. "There you go, son. Birthday present."

Mum laughed and shook her head. "You're crazy," she said, and Steve kissed her again.

I reached out and touched Zac's hand for the first time, and his small fingers closed round mine, tight and strong.

****

I never saw the ghost again.

Barrington Stoke would like to thank all its readers for commenting on the manuscript before publication and in particular:

Trish Babtie
Alex Barnes
Jackie Brown
Robert Brown
Christopher Codonna
Clare Cox
Edward Devine
Julia Donaldson
Gary Ferla
Scott Fisher
Gillian Fraser
Jessica Howarth
Margaret Hubbard
Rebecca Anne Kenney
Siobhan Kinnon
Desmond Kirwan

Lauren Macmillan
Carla McHugh
Gemma McKenzie
Claire Murray
Derek O'Donnell
Darren Parton
Steven Ramage
Kerry Anne Reid
Joanne Riddell
Nicola Rodgers
Kirsty Rolland
James Russell
Mark Sideserf
James Sweeney
Sarah Jane Thomson

Become a Consultant!

Would you like to give us feedback on our titles before they are published? Contact us at the address below – we'd love to hear from you!

E-mail: info@barringtonstoke.co.uk
Website: www.barringtonstoke.co.uk

If you loved this book, why don't you read ...

Wings

by James Lovegrove

ISBN 1-842991-93-0

Az dreams of being like everyone else. In the world of the Airborn that means growing wings. It seems impossible, but with an inventor for a father, who knows?

You can order *Wings* directly from our website at
www.barringtonstoke.co.uk

If you loved this book, why don't you read ...

Ship of Ghosts

by Nigel Hinton

ISBN 1-842991-92-2

Mick's desperate to go to sea, just like the dad he never saw. Now he thinks his dreams are coming true at last. But his adventures turn into nightmares as he slowly finds out about a terrible secret ... what did happen on the Ship of Ghosts?

You can order *Ship of Ghosts* directly from our website at **www.barringtonstoke.co.uk**